The World According to
ELMO

A Story of Health and Safety Tips

By Liza Alexander
Illustrated by Joe Ewers

Featuring Jim Henson's Sesame Street Muppets

A SESAME STREET / GOLDEN PRESS BOOK
Published by Western Publishing Company, Inc.,
in conjunction with Children's Television Workshop.

© 1989 Children's Television Workshop. Sesame Street Muppet Characters © 1989 Muppets, Inc. All rights reserved. Printed in the U.S.A. No part of this book may be reproduced or copied in any form without written permission from the publisher. Sesame Street®, the Sesame Street sign, and Sesame Street GET READY are trademarks and service marks of Children's Television Workshop. All other trademarks are the property of Western Publishing Company, Inc. Library of Congress Catalog Card Number: 88-51565 ISBN: 0-307-13111-4/ ISBN: 0-307-63111-7 (lib. bdg.)   A B C D E F G H I J K L M

"Hello!" said Elmo to Ernie and Bert on the steps of 123 Sesame Street. "Where are you fellows going? Aren't we having a tea party today?"

"We sure are," said Ernie. "Bert and I are just going out to get a few goodies."

"Make yourself at home while we're gone!" added Bert.

"Bye-bye," said Elmo.

Inside, Elmo looked around and wondered where to make himself at home first. He stepped into the bathroom.

"This shiny room is a good place to start!" said Elmo.

He took a toothbrush off the rack. "What's this short skinny thing? I know! A short skinny thing is a pencil!"

Elmo sat on the floor and unrolled a strip of toilet paper.

"E-L-M-O," he said. "Elmo." He tried to write on the toilet paper with the toothbrush handle, but nothing happened.

Elmo hung the toothbrush in its rack and grabbed a bar of soap. "Clock," said Elmo. "What time is it? Ticktock. Ticktock." He shook the bar of soap.

"Hmph. No ticktock. Strange clock."

A tube of toothpaste caught Elmo's eye. "Horn!" he
said. "Hurray!"

Elmo put the end of the tube in his mouth and
blew. He huffed and puffed with all his might, but he
couldn't get the toothpaste to toot.

"Forget it! This horn won't blow."

Next Elmo picked up Bert's hairbrush. "Roller skate!" he said. Elmo stepped on the hairbrush. He slid his foot forward, but the hairbrush stayed put.

"Wheee!" he yelled, pushing harder, but the hairbrush wouldn't roll.

"Time to take a rest," said Elmo with a yawn. "What a comfy little pillow!" Elmo sat down on Bert's bath sponge.

"Ooowee!" he shouted. "This pillow is too scratchy!"

Elmo spied Ernie's back scrubber. He swung the scrubber like a racket.

"Yay!" he yelled. "Now I need a ball!"

"I found a ball!" Elmo cried and grabbed a lemon from a bowl of fruit in the living room. He tossed it up in the air and whacked it with the back of the scrubber.

"Thwack!" said Elmo, but the lemon didn't swoosh through the air and it didn't bounce.

"Now I'll play the drum," said Elmo as he picked
up a melon from the bowl of fruit. He placed it
between his knees.

"Babaloo! Babaloo!" he yelled. Elmo beat the melon
with his hands.

"Blop, blop!" went the melon.

"Lousy drum," thought Elmo.

Bert's barbell in the corner looked interesting to Elmo.

He jumped on top of it and shouted, "Go, bike, go! Zoom, zoom!"

But the barbell wouldn't go anywhere.

The front doorbell jangled. "Jing-a-ling-a-ding-ding!" Ernie and Bert came in with the Count and Countess, who were invited to tea.

"We're back!" said Bert.

"Good!" gasped Elmo. "I was going nowhere fast on your bike."

"Elmo," said Bert, "that is not a bike! Look! There are no wheels and there's no seat. You were sitting on my barbell.

"See? I lift it up and down to build up my muscles and make me strong."

"Ernie, this ball doesn't bounce."

"Silly Elmo!" said Ernie. "That's a lemon, not a ball. It is for our Monster Spice tea!"

"Then what do you hit with the racket?" asked Elmo.

"That's not a racket," said Ernie. "That's a back scrubber. You use it in the bathtub to scrub your back and keep your fur clean."

The Countess set the table for the tea party.
"Shall I play the drum for you?" asked Elmo. He began to pound the melon with his hands. "Babaloo! Babaloo!"
"Blop, blop," went the drum.
"This drum is a dud!" said Elmo.

"That is a melon," said the Countess, "not a drum. Here, Elmo dear, give it to me. Fruit is for eating, not for playing! The melon and these lemons are full of vitamins that will help make us healthy."

"Oh!" said Elmo. "No wonder the melon didn't make much noise."

In the bathroom, Bert began to clean up Elmo's mess. "What has been happening here?" asked Bert. "Why was my bath sponge on the floor?"

"You mean your pillow, Bert? It's very scratchy."

"It's not a pillow," said Bert. "It's my bath sponge."

"How come you have only one roller skate?" asked Elmo. He scooted the hairbrush. "Swoosh!"

"That's my hairbrush, Elmo, not a roller skate. I use it to brush the tangles out of my hair, but now I have to wash it first."

"You need a new clock, Bert," said Elmo. "This one
has no ticktock."

"Little Elmo, this is a bar of soap, not a clock!
Watch! When I mix the soap with water, it makes
suds that wash off the dirt."

Bert held the soap under the water and washed
his hairbrush.

"Come and get it!" called Ernie. "It's teatime!"
Elmo and Bert joined the others around the table.
The Countess poured the tea into pretty little cups.
The Count passed around plates that held fat slices
of melon, chocolate chip cookies, and cupcakes with
gooey icing.

"Dig in!" said Elmo. "Yum, yum!"

Soon only cookie crumbs were left.
"Excuse me," said the Count. "I must brush my fangs after every meal!"
"Oh, may I watch?" asked Elmo.
"Of course," answered the Count.

"This pencil doesn't write," said Elmo, pointing to the toothbrush.

"Elmo, Elmo!" scolded the Count. "That is not a pencil. It is a toothbrush for cleaning teeth." The Count pulled his own toothbrush from his pocket. "I carry my Fango-pay toothbrush with me wherever I go."

The Count unscrewed the cap from Bert's toothpaste.

"Oh, is that how you play the horn?" asked Elmo. "I couldn't get it to toot!"

"Tsk-tsk!" said the Count. "This is not a horn. It is a tube of toothpaste. Watch how I squeeze toothpaste on my toothbrush before I brush. The toothpaste helps prevent cavities!"

The Count brushed his fangs and rinsed the toothpaste from his mouth.

"Time to go, little Elmo," said the Countess when the Count and Elmo returned from the bathroom.

"Thank you very much, Ernie and Bert," said Elmo. "I had a lovely time!"

"You're very welcome!" said Bert. And everybody said their good-byes.

Out on the sidewalk, Elmo reached up and took the Count's hand. "I do know what *this* is for!" sang Elmo happily. "Crossing street! Crossing street! A grown-up's hand! Don't leave home without it!"

"That's right, darling Elmo," said the Countess, laughing. She took Elmo's other hand. The Count and Countess and the furry little monster waited for the light to change from red to green. When the sign said "Walk," they looked both ways to make sure no cars were coming. Then, all holding hands, they crossed Sesame Street together, safe and sound.